Odds 'n' Ends
Alvy

story by **John Frank**

pictures by **G. Brian Karas**

Four Winds Press ❋ *New York*

Maxwell Macmillan Canada *Toronto* **Maxwell Macmillan International** *New York* *Oxford* *Singapore* *Sydney*

Library of Congress Cataloging-in-Publication Data   Frank, John.   Odds 'n' Ends Alvy / story by John Frank ; pictures by G. Brian Karas.—1st ed.   p.   cm.   Summary: Alvy, who likes to make strange new inventions, transforms his school desk into a motorized vehicle and goes for a wild ride.   ISBN 0-02-735675-2 [1. Inventions—Fiction.]   I. Karas, G. Brian, ill.   II. Title.   III. Title: Odds and ends Alvy.   PZ7.F8512Od 1993   [E]—dc20   92-27151

To my Odds 'n' Ends Uncle Moe
—G.B.K.

For Margaret,
who knew it could be built
—J.F.

ALVY FLYNN sat in the back row of Mrs. Potter's class. Alvy never said much, but the other kids liked to gather around his desk anyway, just to watch what he was doing. That's because Alvy was always inventing things. Whenever he finished a school assignment, he'd reach behind his desk for a cardboard box he kept filled with odds and ends. Then he'd start assembling the odds and ends into all kinds of strange new inventions.

It was no wonder he was known around school as Odds 'n' Ends Alvy.

One day Alvy reached into the cardboard box and began attaching odds and ends to the desk itself. His best friends Ethan and Tammy exchanged puzzled looks. Alvy had made hundreds of inventions, but he had never done anything like this. Since Alvy never said much, though, Ethan and Tammy simply scratched their heads and waited to see what would happen.

When Alvy had finished, his desk looked very, very

different.

As Ethan and Tammy and the rest of Alvy's classmates stood around admiring Alvy's unusual new desk, the recess bell *rrrrrang*. But instead of getting in line to go to the playground, Alvy *grabbed* hold of a handle that dangled from his desk by a short piece of rope. He gave the handle a *swift* **tug**.

The desk *jerk*ed suddenly, then started to shake. It *coughed* and sssssssssputtered.

It

With a soft *click* Alvy buckled a seat belt across his waist. He reached around the side of his desk and cupped his hand over a long lever. Taking a deep b r e a t h, he pulled the lever S L O W L Y toward himself.

All at once a giant **roar** filled the room. "LOOK OUT!" yelled Ethan. With a loud **squeeeeal** of rubber, Alvy and his desk *lunged* forward and sped down the aisle.

Alvy steered his desk frantically through the room, **HONK**ing his horn. *Beep, beep!* Students *dove* for cover. Alvy careened around a table, nearly *toppling* the fish tank.

And before anyone knew it, Alvy was out the door, shifting gears wildly as he *raced* down the hall.

At the far end of the building stood Mr. Stone, the school principal. Mr. Stone spent most of his time telling students not to run in the halls. When he spotted Alvy speeding toward him, he held up his palms and announced,

"ALVY FLYNN, THIS HALLWAY IS FOR WALKING ONLY!"

Alvy tried to veer out of the way, *but he was just going* *too fast*. Mr. Stone was FLUNG from his feet and sent

somersaulting

onto his **rear end**.

Alvy SHOT through the hallway door

and ZOOMED out onto the playground.

Beep, beep!

Alvy raced across the blacktop, dodging the sandbox and the swings and the games of hopscotch and foursquare. The first-grade teachers chased after him, **blow**ing their whistles furiously. But by the time they'd caught up to where they had last seen him, Alvy was *screech*ing out of the playground and into the street.

Cars skidded and brakes squealed as drivers turned their heads to gape at Alvy *whizzing* by.

Strolling citizens scurried like startled rabbits as Alvy rounded a curve and sped down the hill.

Beep, beep!

Va·Va·Voom
UNDERWEAR
COMPANY,
UNLIMITED

On the next block, by a big orange CAUTION sign, three city workers stared down into an open manhole. They were hard at work trying to decide who would get to climb down the hole first.

"You go first," said one of the workers. "I'm afraid of the dark."

"No, you go first," said another worker. "There might be alligators swimming around at the bottom."

"No, *you* go first," said the third worker. "It smells funny down there."

Beep, beep!

The three workers looked up and saw Alvy hurtling toward them.
"*ME* first!" they all yelled at once. A loud *SPLASH* sounded
from deep in the ground as Alvy *zoomed* by overhead.

Down the road a strong man was lifting weights in a second-floor gym. He stood by a window as he grunted so people on the street below could admire his **GIGANTIC** muscles.

Beep, beep! The strong man caught a glimpse of Alvy's desk *zip*ping by.

The strong man
was so astonished,
he let go of the dumbbell
in his hand.
It landed **SMACK**
on his big toe.

"OUCH—ACHE!
OUCH—ACHE!"
yelled the strong man,
hopping around
on one foot.

"EARTHQUAKE!
EARTHQUAKE!"
yelled the people
downstairs as
the building
trembled
from all that hopping.

Alvy kept going. Suddenly from up ahead came the rumble of motorcycles. A gang of bikers was **swarming** out of an alley like bats from a cave. They FANNED out in formation, filling three lanes as they headed down the avenue. One of the bikers glanced over his shoulder at Alvy and *snarled*. Alvy reached down and tightened his seat belt.

Beep, beep!

Alvy *BARRELED* through the motorcycles like a bowling ball scattering tenpins! Rasping engines and **grinding** gears drowned out the bikers' confused shouts, and the air grew thick with burning rubber and oily exhaust.

"After him!" hollered the leader of the gang.

Scowls on their faces, the bikers gunned their throttles and stormed down the street. The angry growl of their engines grew LOUDER and LOUDER. They were closing in on Alvy!

Alvy clenched a fist around the lever. When the first motorcycle was so close it was nearly touching him, Alvy gave the lever a YANK. There was a sudden roar, and Alvy SHOT FORWARD and rocketed down the road.

"HEY! Where can we get some wheels like that?"

Alvy DARTED down a narrow side street, then finally began to s l o w   d o w n. He coasted to a stop. Leaving his engine running, he bounded up the stairs of No. 87 and rattled a key in the front-door lock.

Alvy pushed open the door and ran down a hallway into the kitchen. There, taped to the refrigerator, was a handwritten message on a small square of paper:

SAVE

REAL DEAL

10¢ off Poochie Chow

Dear Alvy,

I'm off to work early. Don't forget to feed Boris before you leave for school.

Love ♡ Mom ♡

A basset hound puppy scampered into the kitchen, wagging his tail and whimpering at Alvy. Alvy crouched down and scratched the dog behind the ears. Then he grabbed a box of food from a cupboard and shook some into the dog's empty bowl. He patted Boris once more on the head, then dashed out the door and jumped behind the wheel.

Off went Alvy again, picking up speed, **snaking** through traffic, gobbling up the miles of road. Suddenly ahead flashed the BLINKING red lights of a railroad crossing. TRAIN PASSING they warned. Alvy *slammed* on his brakes—but he couldn't stop in time! As the distance shrank between Alvy and the thundering train, he *grabbed* the lever with both hands and *PULLED* it with all his might. The desk lunged forward, and Alvy was thrown back in his seat.

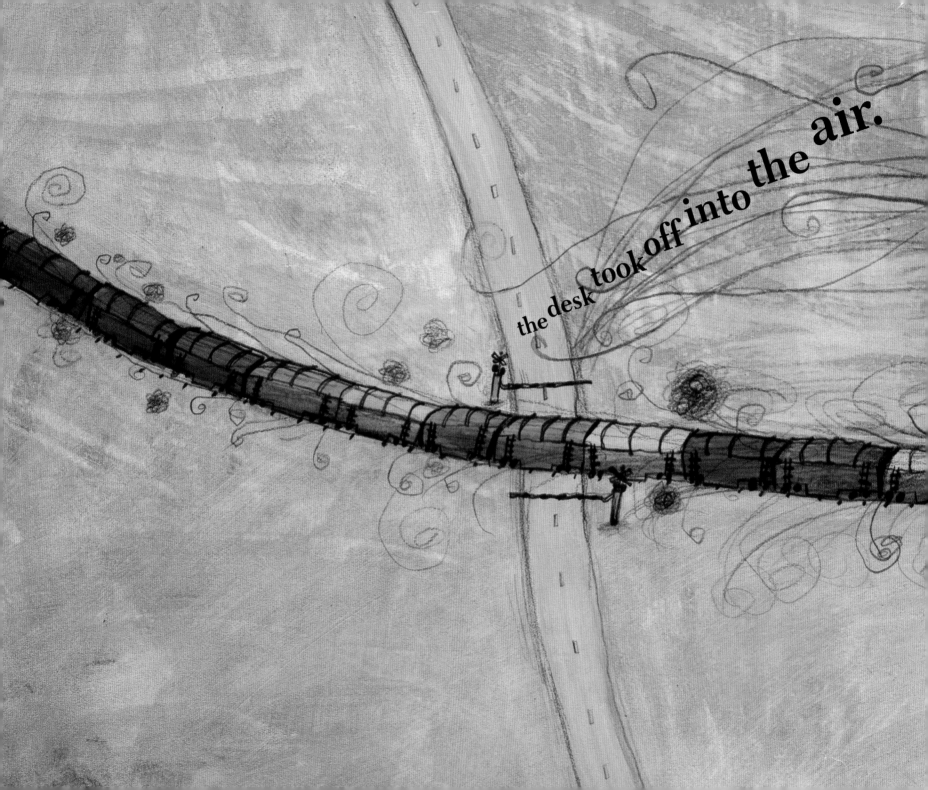

the desk took off into the air.

Alvy soared high above the ground, past the treetops, beyond the roofs of the tallest buildings.

In the distance below he spotted his school.

Nudging the lever forward, Alvy banked his desk across the sky and headed in for a landing. He **g l i d e d** down onto the playground, cruised across the blacktop to the building, and chugged down the long hall. Finally reaching the entrance to his classroom, he turned through the doorway and rolled to a stop in the back row. Cheers and applause erupted from the class. Ethan and Tammy dropped their books and rushed up to their friend. "Alvy!" they exclaimed.

"You're back!"

Alvy looked up with surprise.

"Of course I'm back," he said quietly. "Recess is over, isn't it?"

And with that, Alvy began taking apart
his invention and putting the odds and ends
back into the box.